# Happy St. Patr TINY!

by Cari Meister

illustrated by Rich Davis

Penguin Workshop

For Koki—CM

To John Paul . . .
thank you for your faithful prayers.
Jesus has His hand on your life!—RD

PENGUIN WORKSHOP
An Imprint of Penguin Random House LLC, New York

Text copyright © 2021 by Cari Meister. Illustrations copyright © 2021 by Richard D. Davis. All rights reserved. Published by Penguin Workshop, an imprint of Penguin Random House LLC, New York. PENGUIN and PENGUIN WORKSHOP are trademarks of Penguin Books Ltd, and the W colophon is a registered trademark of Penguin Random House LLC. Manufactured in China.

Visit us online at www.penguinrandomhouse.com.

Library of Congress Cataloging-in-Publication Data is available upon request.

ISBN 9780593097434 (pbk)        10 9 8 7 6 5 4 3 2
ISBN 9780593097441 (hc)         10 9 8 7 6 5 4 3 2 1

It's St. Patrick's Day!

To celebrate, Tiny and I are going to a party in the park where there will be a parade, a costume contest, and a scavenger hunt.

What should
we wear, Tiny?

You can wear this
fancy dog collar and
this big hat.

I will wear these
tights and green
shorts, and this hat
and red beard.

# We look like real leprechauns!

When we get to the park, the parade starts.

There are musicians playing bagpipes, a row of St. Patrick's Day floats, Irish dancers, and more.

Some people dressed as leprechauns throw golden chocolate coins. I run to pick them up, but when I come back, Tiny is gone!

"Tiny! Where are you?" I call out. But I cannot see him.

Tiny is usually easy to find, but not today.

Finally, I find him. He's standing onstage with a ribbon pinned to his hat. He's won fourth place in the costume contest!

"Congratulations, Tiny!" I yell.

When the contestants come down from the stage, a girl in an Irish wolfhound costume looks happy to see me.

"Is this your dog?" she asks. "He's been following me everywhere. He's nice, but his drool is getting all over my costume."

I apologize, then let Tiny say goodbye.
Together we head off to the scavenger hunt.

A man dressed as a leprechaun is giving instructions.

"Follow each clue on the path. The first one to find the pot of gold wins. Are we ready to start?" the leprechaun asks.

"Yes!" we all shout.

"Woof!" says Tiny.

"May the luck of the Irish be with you!" he says as we all run to the first clue.

The first clue is easy to find. It's stuck on a tree.
It says:

"You'll find Clue Number Two on something that's
blue."

I scan the park and see three blue things: the slide, a door to the restroom, and a signpost.

Tiny and I decide to go to the slide. Some kids are already there. They don't see a clue, so they leave and run to the signpost. I start to follow them, but Tiny sniffs something under the slide.

When I crawl under to investigate, I spot the shamrock!

"You'll find Clue Number Three on something that's green," it reads.

I look around the park. So many things are green! I'm about to check out the merry-go-round when Tiny takes off.

"Tiny, come back!" I yell.

But Tiny has spotted the girl in the Irish wolfhound costume and won't listen.

When I finally catch up to them, I realize that we are far away from the scavenger hunt.

"Sorry," I say to the girl. "He just really likes you."

That's when I see that she's crying.

"What's the matter?" I ask.

"I lost my shoe," the girl says. "I was playing in the sandbox and so I took my shoes off, and when I went to put them back on, only one was there. They're new shoes and I'm so sad."

"We can help you find your lost shoe," I say.
"Tiny's good at finding things."

We search for the girl's shoe. We look by the bench.

We look by the tree.

We look and
look, but we
cannot find it.
We are about to
give up, when—

"Woof!" Tiny calls.

Tiny has found the shoe, and the next clue!

"Thank you," the girl says, giving Tiny a big kiss.

"You are the luckiest boy I know," the girl tells me. "You have the best dog ever!"

I start to read the clue on the shamrock.

"Keep going! The pot is very close—"

All of a sudden, we hear a joyous roar up ahead.

Someone else has found the pot of gold!

"That's okay," I tell Tiny. "I'm still the luckiest kid around—I have you!"

Happy St. Patrick's Day, Tiny!